Buttons Visits

MW01045930

by Lynn Groth

illustrated by Tammie Lyon

NORTHWESTERN PUBLISHING HOUSE
Milwaukee, Wisconsin

Special thanks to Paul Burmeister for his art and story direction.

Scripture is taken from the HOLY BIBLE, NEW INTERNATIONAL VERSION®. Copyright © 1973, 1978, 1984 by International Bible Society. Used by permission of Zondervan Publishing House. All rights reserved.

The "NIV" and "New International Version" trademarks are registered in the United States Patent and Trademark Office by International Bible Society. Use of either trademark requires the permission of International Bible Society.

Library of Congress Control Number: 2002100798
Northwestern Publishing House
1250 N. 113th St., Milwaukee, WI 53226-3284
© 2003 Northwestern Publishing House
www.nph.net
Published 2003
Printed in the United States of America
ISBN 0-8100-1332-0

 Printed with soy inks on recycled paper.

Buttons is a little bear
Who's growing, just like you.
He wants to learn so many things.
And you can learn them too!

As you turn each page, please look—
A button may hide there.
And listen as the story tells
About God's love and care.

This is love for God: to obey his commands.

1 John 5:3

Buttons woke up with a smile. It was Saturday morning.
"Super! I get to go to Grandma's house today," he said.

Buttons got dressed and hopped into the car with his mom and dad. "Let's go!" said Buttons as he held Floppy the Bunny, his favorite toy.

Grandma was sitting on her porch waiting for them.

She had a ball and bat next to her. "Hi, Buttons," she said. "Ready to hit a few?"

"Super!" said Buttons as he hugged his Grandma. He loved to have Grandma pitch to him. She knew just how fast to throw the ball so that Buttons could hit it.

"Obey Grandma while we're gone," said Buttons' dad.

Buttons and Grandma played ball for a long time. Once Buttons hit the ball so hard that it rolled into the street. Buttons began to run after it.

"Stop!" shouted Grandma. "I will help you get the ball, Buttons. Never, never run into the street after a ball."

After getting the ball safely, Grandma said, "Let's go have lunch in the backyard." On the way Buttons began to climb up her woodpile.

"No, Buttons!" said Grandma. "I've told you not to do that.
If the logs begin to roll, you'll fall."

When they got to the backyard, Buttons was surprised to see a tent. "Super! Did you make that tent? Oh, thank you, Grandma!" he said.

Buttons and Grandma crawled into the tent. Grandma had sandwiches, cookies, grapes, and juice waiting for them inside.

After lunch, Grandma took Buttons inside for a bath. Buttons liked baths at Grandma's house because she always put lots of bubbles in the tub. Grandma spread bubbles on Buttons' face and said, "Buttons, you have a beard!"

Then Buttons lay down in the tub and covered his whole body with bubbles. "Where is Buttons?" called Grandma.

"Here I am!" shouted Buttons as he jumped up and down.

"Buttons! Don't jump in the tub," warned Grandma. "We've talked about that before."

When bathtime was over, Grandma let Buttons play with an old train. "Your grandpa played with this train when he was a boy," said Grandma.

"Super!" said Buttons. Then he hooked the cars together and gave Floppy a ride on the train.

Grandma sat nearby, sewing up a hole in Buttons' sock. "Remember how I told you not to touch the needles," said Grandma.

Too late! Buttons had already grabbed one. "Ouch!" he cried.

"Buttons! You need to listen! Come here, and I'll help your paw feel better," said Grandma as she washed Buttons' paw and put a bandage on it. *Hmmm . . .* thought Grandma.

"Buttons, I'd like to tell you about a man named Noah who loved God and obeyed him."

Grandma sat on the couch and pulled Buttons up on her lap. He hugged Floppy as Grandma read these words from her Bible story book:

A long time ago, the world was full of people who did not believe in God or obey him.

But Noah believed in God and loved him. So did Noah's family.
One day God told Noah, "The people on earth don't love and obey me anymore. I am going to send lots and lots of water that will cover the whole earth. Build a big boat called an ark. Fill the ark with animals. I will save you, your family, and the animals inside the ark."

Right away Noah did what God said. Noah showed that he loved God by obeying him. Noah built the ark just the way God told him to make it.

After Noah, his family, and the animals were safe inside the ark, God closed the door.

Then God sent lots and lots of water to cover the earth. It rained for many days, but the ark floated safely on the water.

When the time was right, God made the water go down, down, down. After many days, the ark landed on a mountain. Noah, his family, and the animals inside the ark were fine. God had saved them!

God put a rainbow in the sky to show that he would never destroy the whole world with water again. Noah and his family continued to love and obey God, and they thanked him for saving them.

Grandma set the book down. She said, "Buttons, as we lie down for a nap today, I hope you will think about showing love to God by obeying him as Noah did."

"And one way to obey God is to obey the people who take care of you," said Grandma.

"Like you, Grandma?" asked Buttons.

"Like me, Buttons," answered Grandma with a smile. "Now, clean up your toys and come for a nap."

Quickly Buttons put the train cars into a box and grabbed Floppy. And just as quickly he ran back and snuggled next to Grandma for his nap.

"I love you, Grandma," said Buttons as he hugged Floppy and fell asleep.

Did you find the buttons
That were hiding here and there?
Someone special has found you.
He gives you love and care.

Jesus is that someone's name.
He lived and died for you.
Trust him, love him, and obey
In all you say and do.